USBORNE HOTSHOTS

TRICK PHOTOGRAPHY

USBORNE HOTSHOTS

TRICK PHOTOGRAPHY

Written by Mandy Ross
Designed by Karen Tomlins

Photographs by Ray Moller

Illustrated by Kathy Ward,
Kim Blundell and Kuo Kang Chen

Series editor: Judy Tatchell
Series designer: Ruth Russell

Models: Tom Ashby, Edward Cheesman, Harry Gibson, Harriet Haslam, Emily Kirby-Jones, Hannah Kirby-Jones, Marina Townsend, Francesca Tyler, Alexander Vines

CONTENTS

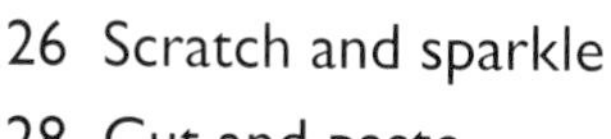

Getting started

This book shows you how to take lots of of exciting trick photos – optical illusions, fakes and tricks of the light. You can take all the pictures without expensive equipment. All you need is a camera, a roll of film, a few everyday objects – and some people who like having their picture taken.

What type of camera?

You can use any type of camera for the trick photographs in this book, even a disposable one. For some photos, you will need to use a flash (see below).

With automatic cameras, you don't have to worry about focusing on your subject or adjusting for different light conditions. The camera does it all for you.

With adjustable cameras, you have more control over the focus and the exposure or light setting (see below). This means that you need to be careful that each of your photos is in focus and well lit.

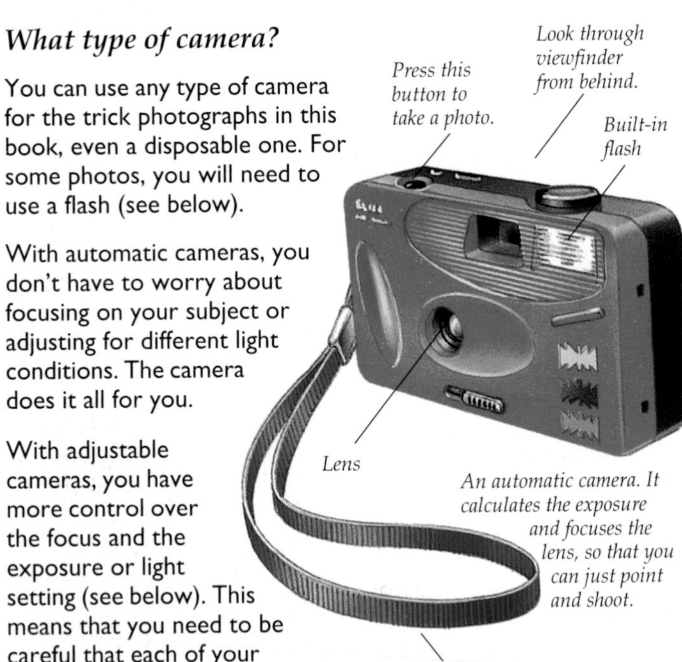

An automatic camera. It calculates the exposure and focuses the lens, so that you can just point and shoot.

Photography words

Here are a few key words for talking about photography.
Exposure: the amount of light entering the camera. If the exposure is right, the picture is neither too dark nor too light.
Flash: a burst of artificial light, used for taking photos when there is not enough natural light.
Focus: if a photo is in focus, it looks sharp. If it looks blurred and fuzzy, it is out of focus.

Film

Film is a layer of thin plastic with a light-sensitive coating. Most cameras take either 35mm film or 110 or 126 cartridge film. If you are not sure which your camera needs, take it into a shop that sells film and ask for advice.*

A roll of 35mm film

Light and flash

Most photography works best in plenty of light. Snapping outdoors in the sunshine makes bright pictures.

Indoors or in the dark, you may need to use a flash to light up your subject. But for some of the trick photos in this book, it is important to avoid using the flash. Where you see this symbol, don't use the flash.

Some cameras have an automatic flash which you can't switch off. If you have one of these, you can block out the flash by covering it with a large blob of reusable sticky stuff, such as Blu-Tack®.

Composing photos

Always think carefully about composition – that is, how the people or objects are arranged in your photo.

Hold the camera vertically for tall, narrow shapes, and horizontally for wide pictures.

Check how much will fit in your photo by looking through the viewfinder.

Only the area inside these border marks will show in the photo.

Try not to cut off heads or bodies accidentally.

With most simple cameras, you must be at least 1.5m (4ft) away from your subject – or your photos will be out of focus.

**Print film – where photos are printed onto paper – is best for the ideas in this book. Ask for average speed film that works well both inside and outside, such as 200 ISO.*

Optical illusions

The camera never lies – or does it? The next eight pages show you how to photograph some amazing optical illusions. Check through the camera that everything is in place before you take the picture.

Leaning skyscraper

You don't need superhuman strength to prop up a skyscraper like this – just clever photography.

Choose a tall building with a clear skyline. Ask a friend to stand at least 20 to 25 paces away from it. She should pretend to push against it. Walk another two paces farther, and squat down as low as you can. Look through the camera. If you are both in the right position, your friend should now seem very tall in relation to the building.

Tilt the camera a little, so the building will look as if it is leaning. Ask your friend to adjust the angle of her hands until they look as though they are pushing against the edge of the building.

Legs extension

For this trick, ask someone to lie down with their legs hidden behind a large umbrella. Ask a second person to sit behind the umbrella, so that their legs stretch out on the other side.

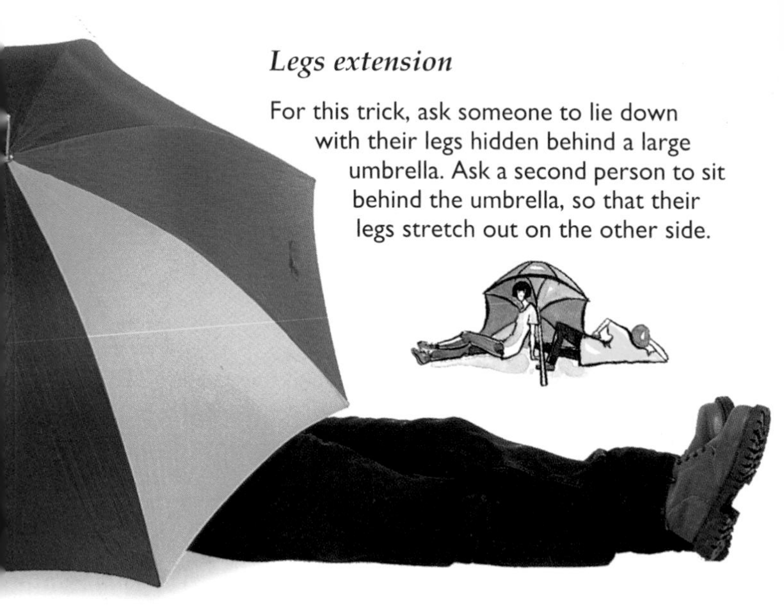

Helping hands

Life would be so much more fun with two pairs of hands – and here's a photo to prove it. You will need two people wearing identical tops. Ask one person to hide behind the other, and push her arms forward under the front person's arms. The person behind should squeeze in tightly, so that only her arms show.

Check that you can't see the head of the person behind.

Make sure each of the four hands has a job to do.

Ask the person in front to hold their arms out wide, so that all four arms show clearly in the final photo.

Balancing books

Find a shelf, wall or gate post that is about the same height as a friend. Pile up a tall stack of books on it. Then, looking through the camera, line up your friend so that her head is just underneath the books. Photographs make images look flat, so it will not show that she is standing a little in front of them.

Ask her to look worried, and to pose as if the books are just starting to wobble.

Arms outstretched as if for stability

One leg is pointing out as if she is trying to regain her balance.

Making a plain background

Lots of optical illusions, like the cartwheeling waiter opposite, work best against a plain background which gives away no clues. To create a white background, trap a plain white sheet over the top of a door. Drape it in a gentle curve so that it doesn't make a fold where it meets the floor. Then ask your subject to stand carefully on the sheet, wearing clean shoes.

Cartwheeling waiter

This cartwheeling waiter has at least one foot firmly on the ground. It's the photo which is upside down, not him.

Tape some plastic or paper cups firmly onto a tray so they won't fall off. Then ask your waiter to hold one arm straight up and stand with his legs wide apart. He could point one foot out, to add to the cartwheeling effect.

With his other hand, he should hold the tray upside down so the cups point to the floor. Position the tray so that the cups hide his hand.

Make sure the waiter's legs are wide apart, as if he is doing a cartwheel.

Your waiter should stand like this when you take the photo.

The cups and straws need to be firmly taped or glued in place.

This hand is hidden, so that it looks as if he is supporting the tray on the flat of his hand – just like a real waiter.

This arm should be stretched up high with the palm facing up, to look as if it is supporting him.

Is it a bird? Is it a plane?

Here's how to turn your friends into flying superheroes. Ask someone to lie on a plain white sheet. Stand or kneel about 1m (3ft) behind his head to take the picture. Then turn the print upside down to display it at a flying angle.

For a basic flying costume, you could make a mask, cape and belt to wear with tracksuit bottoms and a matching sweatshirt.

This arm points up toward the camera.

Cardboard mask covered in kitchen foil.

This knee is raised to give the impression of movement.

One leg is stretched out with the foot pointing away from the camera.

Position the cape to add to the zooming effect.

Ask your subject to tilt his head back and look at the camera.

Thumbelina

This tiny figure seems to be balancing on a girl's hand. In fact the girl is near the camera, while "Thumbelina" sits in the distance, carefully lined up. Take this picture outdoors as the subjects are too far away to use a flash.

This distance should be around three paces.

This distance should be at least ten paces, and could be more.

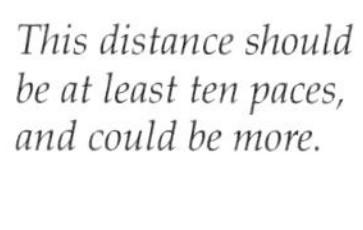

Look through the camera to line up the tiny person on the girl's hand.

This person stands or sits, holding out her hand and looking ahead.

Line this person up so that she stands or sits on the hand. The farther away she is, the smaller she will seem.

Ask the nearer person to gaze just a little above her hand. Then in the photo she seems to look directly at "Thumbelina".

Double trouble

To create this two-headed creature, you need a long mirror, preferably without a frame. A mirror on a hinged wardrobe door is ideal. Take this picture in plenty of light, but don't use a flash, as it may be reflected in the mirror.

Ask someone to stand with the mirror down the middle of their body, and their head poked out at an angle. If they hold one leg out, it will look as though they are floating in mid-air. Look through your camera until you see the best image.

Off with her head

Now you can cut off someone's head without spilling a drop of blood. Ask a friend to stand sideways to you, and then flop her head back and sideways away from you as far as she can. You should squat or kneel, getting as low as possible until her head is hidden from view behind her shoulders.

Strong shoulders

Here's how to fake these sensationally strong shoulders.

Ask an adult to stand on a stool. Position a child in front of the stool. The child should crouch or sit, so that the stool's legs are hidden behind her body, and its top is level with her shoulders. Now it should look as though the adult is standing on her shoulders.

You will need to be quite a distance away to take this shot. It may work best outdoors where there is plenty of space.

Hold the camera vertically so that the picture fills the frame.

The child should hold her hands on her shoulders, palms facing up. You could ask her to grimace, as if she is bearing a heavy load. Ask the adult to hold his arms straight out, and to look as if he is struggling to keep his balance.

Fantastic fakes

The history of photography is full of fakes. You probably won't fool the experts, but you might baffle your friends and family with these ideas for fake photos.

Faking a flying saucer

Unidentified flying objects – or UFOs for short – make the headlines every few years. On these two pages are some different techniques for faking photos of vehicles from outer space.

You can use the templates on the right for your fake photos. Either stick the shapes on the inside of a window (see below), or shine a flashlight through a UFO-shaped hole cut out of cardboard, to make a luminous UFO, as shown opposite.

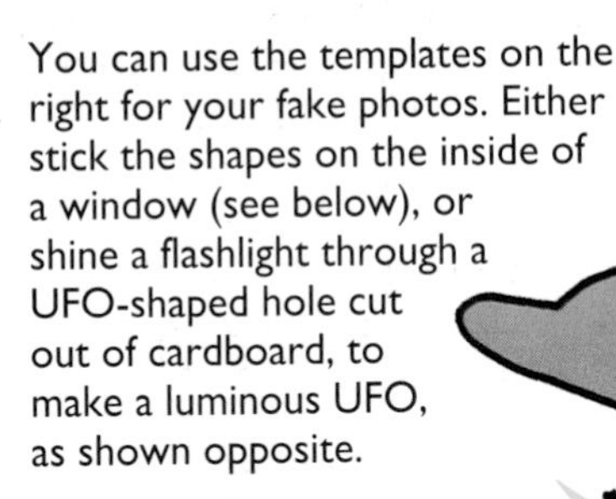

This menacing UFO was photographed indoors. Cut out a UFO shape from dark paper, using the templates above. Stick it onto a clean window. Stand only a pace away from the window to snap, so that the UFO looks blurred, as if in motion. Don't use a flash.

For this fake, you need a metal lampshade or a saucepan lid. Lie down in an open space. Ask someone to throw the "UFO" over you (making sure that it does not fall on you). Snap the object against the sky. Try to include buildings or trees in the photo, to give a sense of scale.

Luminous UFO

To create a glowing UFO, you will need a large flashlight, with a diameter of at least 5cm (2in). Take this picture indoors at dusk, when there is still just a little light left in the sky. Don't use a flash.

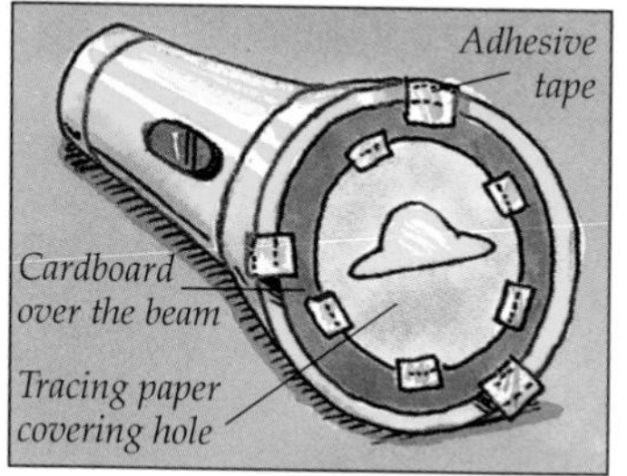

On cardboard, draw around the top of the flashlight. Cut out the circle, and cut a UFO-shaped hole from it. Cover the hole with tracing paper. Tape the cardboard over the beam.

Switch off the lights and ask someone to shine the flashlight at a window. Looking through the camera, position yourself so that the UFO's reflection seems to hover in the sky outside.

Here is the photo of a UFO glowing in the evening sky. The red glow at the bottom is a streetlight which has just come on.

Ghostly reflections

This ghostly snapshot was taken indoors, facing a window. The photo shows someone draped in a white sheet, reflected in the window.

Look for light conditions where you can see both the reflection and the view through the window. Switch off all the lights in the room. Use the flash, and stand at an angle to the window to take the picture. Then the photo will not show the reflection of the flash.

Felt-tip fake

Even if sea monsters really exist, no one has managed to take a clear photo of one. You can draw your own fake monster with felt-tip pens on a photo of the sea or a lake. You will need to take care not to smudge the ink until it is completely dry.

The Cottingley fairies

Elsie Wright was only 15 when she photographed her young cousin, Frances Griffiths, playing with fairies near their home in Cottingley, Yorkshire. The photographs, published in 1920, fascinated the public and puzzled experts around the world. Were the fairies real? If not, how did the girls fake the photographs?

Elsie and Frances kept their secret for over 60 years. Only in 1983 did they reveal how they had painted pictures of fairies, cut them out and pinned them in place using hatpins.

You can paint your own fake fairies – or use a Christmas tree fairy if you have one. Choose a leafy spot and position the fairies carefully among the leaves, hiding any pins or sticky tape behind the leaves. Or you can hang them from branches using fishing line, which will not show in the photo.

The fairies below, shown from behind, have been cut out with cardboard tabs on their feet, and then pinned in position.

Portrait gallery

Why settle for boring old mugshots? The next four pages suggest some weird and whacky portrait ideas. Remember not to stand closer than about 1.5m (4ft) or your portraits will be out of focus.

Big feet

Objects near the camera look larger than distant objects. This effect, called foreshortening, can make unusual portraits. Ask someone to hold one foot out toward the camera. Take the picture at the moment when his foot is lined up with his face. Take this picture in bright light, and make sure that his foot kicks 1.5m (4ft) from the camera.

Underlighting

After dark, get a friend to shine a flashlight up under his chin. Don't use a flash. For a spooky effect, ask him to make a scary face.

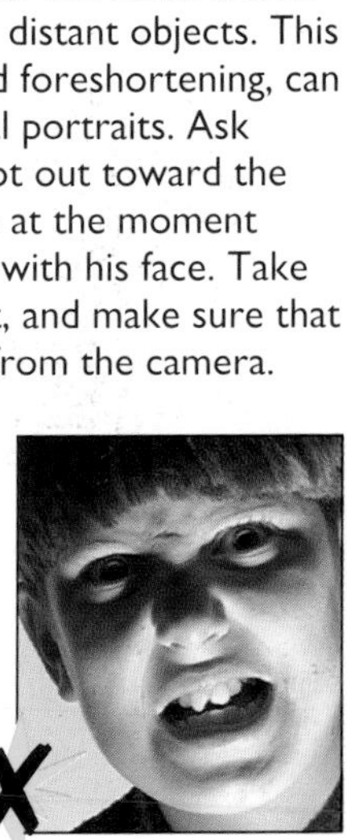

Hot hair

Create this startling effect by asking someone to stand right in front of a desk lamp which is pointing straight ahead. Look through the camera, and move around until her head blocks out the light, but is surrounded by rays. Don't use a flash, as it will cancel out the lamp's rays.

Silhouettes

You can create striking silhouettes by taking photos which are lit from behind. Cover a sunny window with tracing paper to create a light, plain background. Ask someone to stand or sit sideways in front of it. Don't use a flash for this photo.

Ask your subject to face sideways for a good profile.

In the photo the person will look dark in front of the bright background.

Finished silhouette

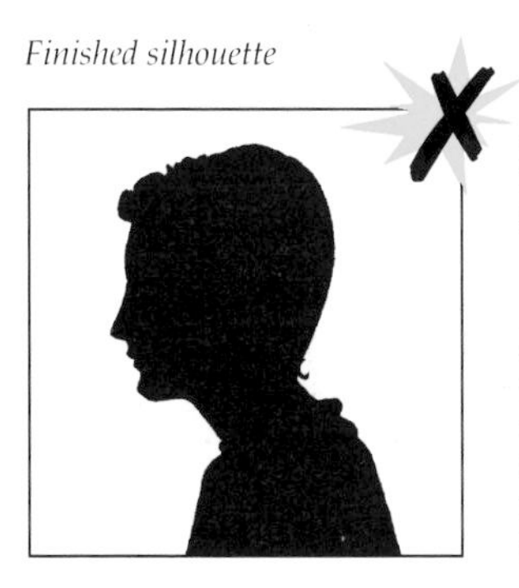

Whacky picture frame

This looks like an ordinary portrait – until you notice that the subject is starting to emerge from the frame.

You will need to cut around the outside of the frame in the finished photo if the arms stick out beyond it. If you can't find a picture frame, you could make one out of cardboard.

This kind of portrait looks best if you take it in front of a plain, bright background.

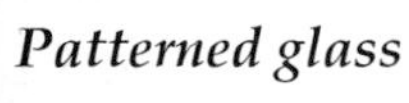

Patterned glass

Try taking portraits through patterned glass, such as the windows in a front door. Take this type of picture in bright sunlight. Ask your subject to stand where the sun shines through the glass, lighting up his or her face. Avoid using a flash.

Watery wobbles

The rounded shapes of clear glass jars and bottles act like distorting lenses. You can use this effect to create warped and wobbly portraits by taking pictures through them.

Fill a clear glass vase with water, and dry its sides. Ask someone to stand with their face very close behind it. Avoid using a flash, as it will reflect on the glass.

For other distortions, you could try taking a picture through a row of bottles or jars of water standing side by side. When your subjects are in position, look through your camera and move around until you see the best distortion. Don't use a flash.

Hair-raising

Ask a long-haired friend to hang upside down, for instance on a climbing frame or swing. She should fold her arms so they don't show in the final photo.

Try to make sure the background is plain for this photo, so it doesn't give away any clues. When the photo is developed, simply turn it upside down.

Mix and match

You will need a few portraits taken straight on, showing people's faces the same size. Cut each face into strips at the same height – below the nose, for instance, or above the eyes.

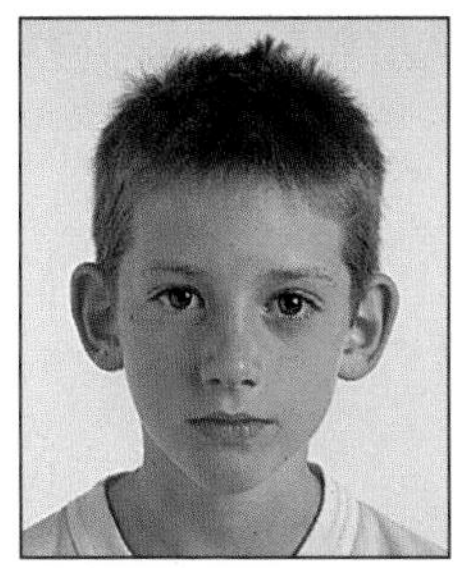

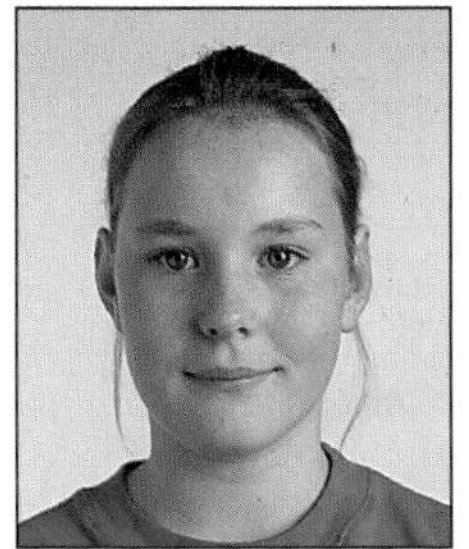

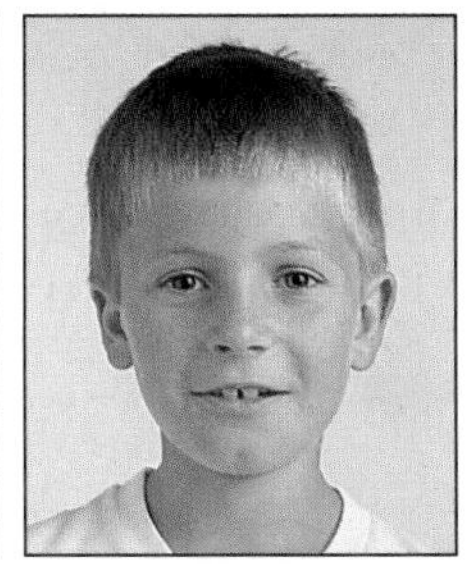

Now you can mix and match to create lots of new faces. This makes a fascinating experiment with members of your family, to find out which features you share.

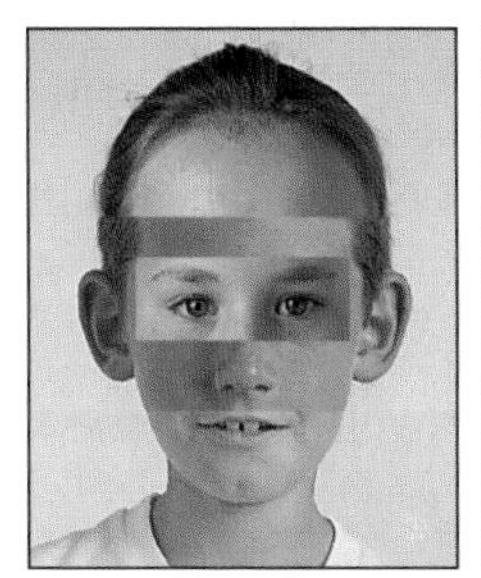

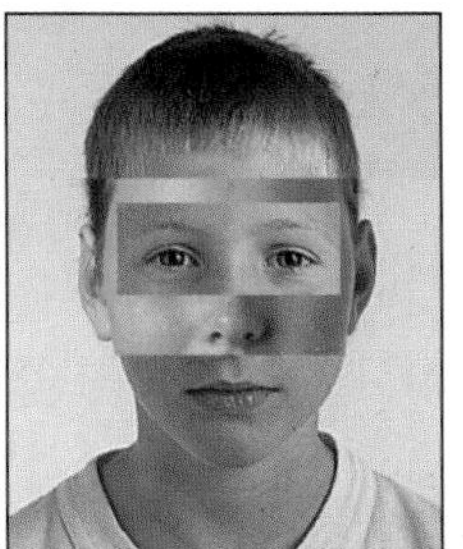

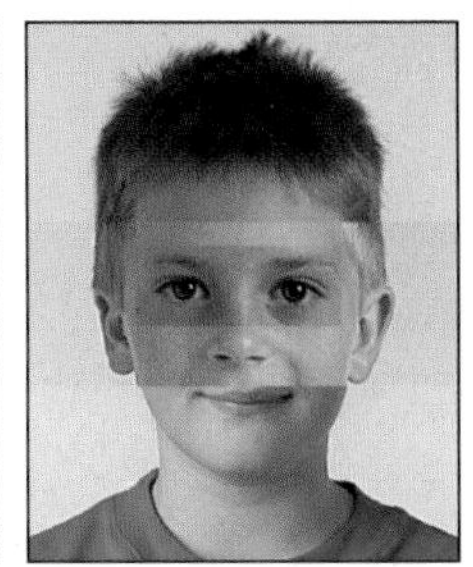

Group photos

Group photos don't have to be straight faced and formal. Here are some lighthearted ideas.

Severed heads

Take this picture outdoors in the dark, using a flash. Ask your subjects to dress in black, and to stand far away from any surface – such as a tree – which may be lit up by the flash. Snap from about four paces away.

Three's a crowd

Here's how to turn just a few friends into a huge crowd. The photo below is made up of eight shots of the same three people. You can adapt this idea for large gatherings, too, by taking pictures of people in small, manageable groups and pasting them together.

1. Ask three people to stand close together in front of a simple background (such as a plain wall). Take their picture.

2. Take several more shots of them in different poses and positions. Hold the camera at the same height each time.

3. Take a print, and cut away the left hand edge, starting from the head of the person on the left and cutting down to their feet.

4. Overlay this on the next shot to look as if the people are standing next to each other. Repeat to make a long line.

Circle of friends

For the striking group portrait on the right, six people lay on the floor with their heads close together. To take this type of picture, you will need to point the camera straight down at the faces. You may need to stand on a chair or even a ladder to get right above them.

For a different viewpoint, you could lie on the ground, and ask everyone to crowd around you looking down into the lens. You will need to use a flash to light up their faces. Ask long-haired people to tie their hair back.

Avoiding red eye

When you take pictures with a flash, your portraits may have a red dot in their eyes. To avoid this effect, called red eye, ask your subject to look slightly above the camera. You can cover red eye on your prints with a dot with a brown felt-tip pen.

Tinted photos

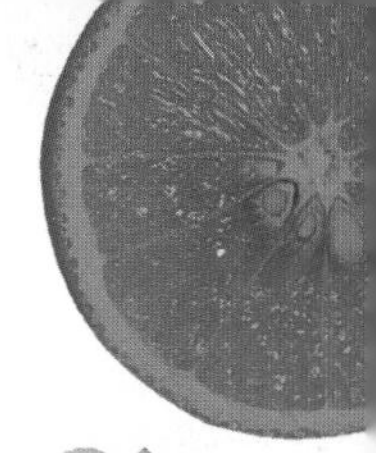

You can use cellophane chocolate wrappers as filters to create tinted photos. Take your filter photos in plenty of light, as the filter will cut down on the light entering the camera.

Never draw or stick anything directly on your lens, as you will not be able to get it clean again.

Making your filter

Cut two circles of cellophane which cover your lens, without sticking out beyond the lens surround. Hold the circles one on top of the other, and lay them over the lens panel. Press tiny blobs of reusable sticky stuff* over the edges to stick them to the camera – not to the lens itself.

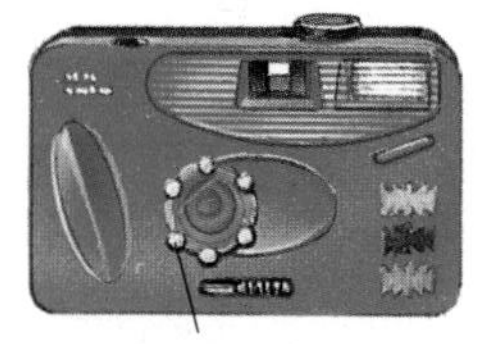

These tiny sticky blobs hold the circles of cellophane in place.

Filters on flash

Indoors, tape your filters over the flash instead of the lens. Through the filter, the flash bathes objects nearby in an intense glow. More distant objects are not affected.

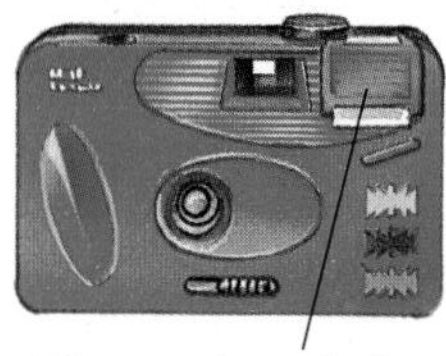

Filter taped over flash

Outdoor filters

Filters work well outdoors, transforming a scene into wintry shades or creating a strange, unearthly atmosphere. Choose light scenes, like snow or trees against a bright sky, for best effects.

**An example of reuseable sticky stuff is* Blu-Tack®.

Funny food

Whoever heard of a purple lemon or a blue tomato? Instead of filters, you can use felt-tip pens to draw on your prints, changing shades or adding patterns. Never draw directly on your lens!

This method lets you work on certain areas of your prints, rather than the whole picture.

Pale shades give an effect like a transparent wash, as you can see on the mushrooms. Dark brown and black look opaque, blocking out the print beneath.

Filters on faces

You can use filters to alter the mood of portraits, like the ones below. Give your friends a sickly tinge by using a green or yellow filter – or a rosy glow with a pink one.

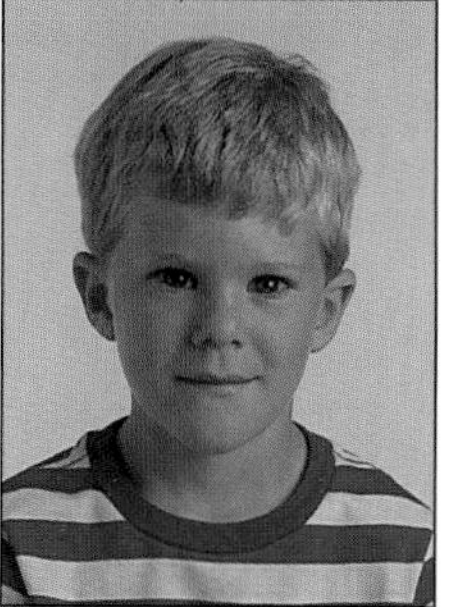

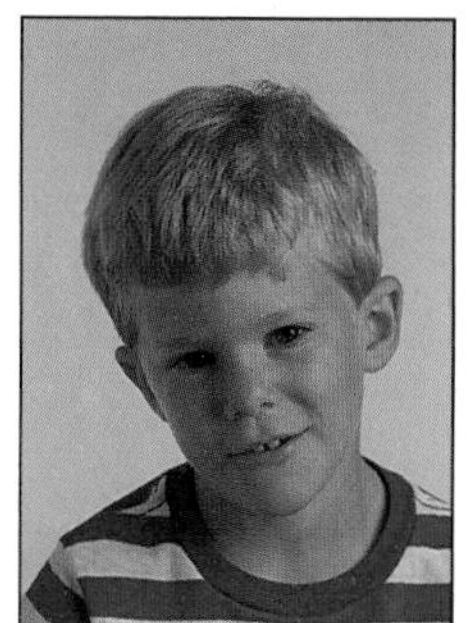

Scratch and sparkle

A photograph is printed by building up layers of chemicals on paper. These two pages show you how to create a sparkly, glowing effect by scratching off the surface layers.

How to scratch and sparkle

It's best to experiment with a photo that you don't want to keep. Remember to ask permission to do this to other people's photos.

Dip a fine paintbrush in warm water, and use it to moisten a small patch of the photograph. Work the water carefully into the surface of the photo.

Using a blunt point, such as a pencil or the wrong end of the paintbrush, scratch gently at the wet surface. You should reveal an orange or gold scratch mark.

Speed of light

Scratching behind this go-kart's wheels gives an effect of earth-scorching speed. The same effect works well for bikes or cars. You could turn people into superhuman athletes by adding scratch and sparkle marks behind their heels.

Spectacular sunsets

In this photo, the ripples on the sea's surface have been scratched off to look like magical reflections of the sun.

You could also create a spectacular sunset by scratching dazzling rays, stars and sparkles all around the setting sun. The effect will look most striking if you find a photo of the sun against a fairly dark sky.

Warning!

With this scratch and sparkle technique, you are scratching away at photographic chemicals, which can be harmful.

Do not let these chemicals touch your skin, and always avoid putting your fingers near your mouth while you are using this technique. Never lick a photo. Make sure you wash your hands thoroughly as soon as you have finished.

Cut and paste

By cutting up photos and sticking them together on another piece of paper, you can build up large, complex pictures that you couldn't take in a single shot. This technique is called *montage* (say "mon-tarj"). It lets you combine photos and magazine pictures in all sorts of ways.

Tower

This picture of a tower is made up of lots of prints of small parts of the building, pasted together to form a larger picture. For this kind of montage, you can just overlay your prints – you don't need to cut them up.

Soaring city

Even in the most exciting city in the world, you won't find a view quite as dramatic as this.

Take or cut out photos of lots of buildings. Plan a design for your montage. Paste the building shapes onto a background, with tall shapes tapering up to the skyline.

The cut edges of a photo look white. You can hide these edges by drawing along them with a felt-tip pen of the right shade.

Human centipede

This montage is made up of several shots of the same person in different poses. Choose one photo to form the base. Then cut out extra arms and legs and stick them down onto the base photo. Here the separate poses are shown above the finished montage.

Juggling heads

This juggling act isn't as gruesome as it looks. Ask someone to pose as if they are juggling, with their arms outstretched, palms facing up. When the photo is developed, cut out the whole figure and then cut the head off.

Paste the body onto a suitable background. Then cut out some more heads from other photos or from magazines. Paste them around the body as if they are being expertly juggled.

Size and scale

Is it a miniature wizard or a giant cat under a spell? By cutting and pasting from two different prints, you can use montage to play with size and scale.

Before you take any photographs, plan or sketch the finished effect you want. Then you can ask your model to pose in the right position.

Frame your work

Don't leave your trick photos hidden in a drawer! It is easy to make a photo frame to display your work in its full glory. You could design the frame to suit the theme of the photo, like the sea monster frame on the right.

Basic photo frame

1. To make a frame, cut out a piece of cardboard about 2cm (1in) larger all the way around than your photo.

2. Cut out a hole in the middle, slightly smaller than the photo. Decorate your frame with paint or felt-tip pens.

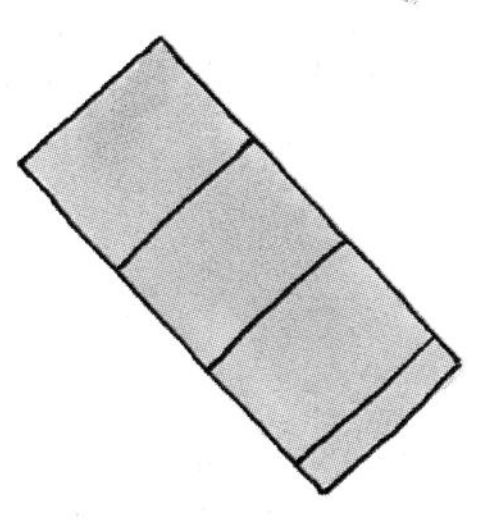

3. To make a stand, draw around your photo on cardboard. Then draw another 2½ oblong shapes beside it.

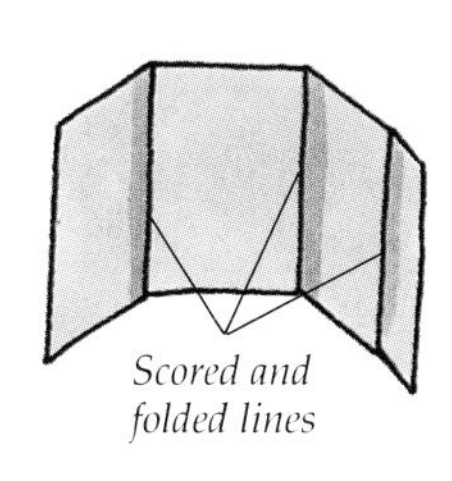

4. Cut out the whole shape. Score by scratching with an old ballpoint pen against a ruler held along each line. Fold the scored lines.

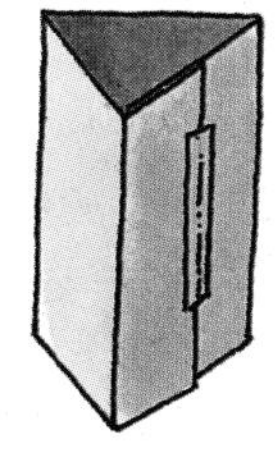

5. Fold and tape the cardboard shape into a triangular tube. This stand will support your frame either standing up or sideways.

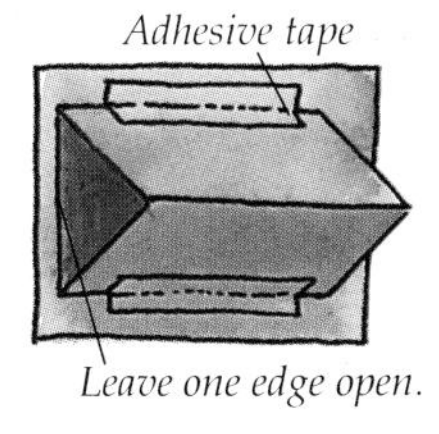

6. Lay the stand in the middle of the frame. Seal three edges with adhesive tape. Slide your photo in through the open edge.

Index

The publishers would like to thank the following for permission to reproduce their photographs in this book: The Brotherton Collection, Leeds University Library (17), Julian Cotton Photo Library (30 bottom left), Renault (5 top left), Alan Ross (5 top right, middle; 16 bottom; 24 bottom; 28 top, bottom).
Additional photographs by Anne Cardale, Chris Gilbert, Tony McConnell and Karen Tomlins.
With thanks to The Band Box (Wolverhampton) Ltd and Grand Prix Karting, Walsall.

This book uses material previously published by Usborne in the *Guide to Photography, Decorating T-shirts, Face Painting* and *Fancy Dress.*
First published in 1996 by Usborne Publishing Ltd, Usborne House, 83-85 Saffron Hill, London EC1N 8RT, England.

First published in America March 1997. UE
Printed in Italy.